I0533016

# THE PRESSING PERIL

# THE PRESSING PERIL

## Or, Nick Carter And The Star Looters

## NICHOLAS CARTER

**WILDSIDE PRESS**

Copyright © 2022 by Wildside Press LLC.
Originally published in *Nick Carter Stories* (1915).
Published by Wildside Press LLC.
wildsidepress.com | bcmystery.com

# INTRODUCTION

Nick Carter is a fictional character who began as a detective series character in 1886 and has appeared in a variety of formats over more than a century. He first appeared in the story paper *New York Weekly* (Vol. 41 No. 46, September 18, 1886) in a 13-week serial, *The Old Detective's Pupil; or, The Mysterious Crime of Madison Square*.

The character was conceived by Ormond G. Smith, the son of one of the founders of Street & Smith, and realized by John R. Coryell. The character proved popular enough to headline its own magazine, *Nick Carter Weekly*. The serialized stories in *Nick Carter Weekly* were also reprinted as stand-alone titles under the New Magnet Library imprint.

By 1915, *Nick Carter Weekly* had ceased publication and Street & Smith had replaced it with *Detective Story Magazine*, which focused on a more varied cast of characters. There was a brief attempt at reviving Carter in 1924–27 in *Detective Story Magazine*, but it was not successful.

In the 1930s, due to the success of *The Shadow* and *Doc Savage*, Street & Smith revived Nick Carter in a pulp magazine (called *Nick Carter Detective Magazine*) that ran from 1933 to 1936. Since the Doc Savage character had basically been given Nick's background, Nick Carter was now recast as a hard-boiled detective. Novels featuring Carter continued to appear through the 1950s, by which time there was also a popular radio show, *Nick Carter, Master Detective,* which aired on the Mutual Broadcasting System network from 1943 to 1955.

*The Pressing Peril* (originally published May 8, 1915 as the lead novel in *Nick Carter Stories*) has been lightly edited to modernize language and punctuation.

Enjoy!

—John Betancourt
Cabin John, Maryland

# THE PRESSING PERIL

# CHAPTER 1

## THE WOMAN WHO VANISHED

"Oh, I say, old top!"

Nick Carter stopped short and looked at the speaker. There was no mistaking his nationality. He was English to the bone. English in aspect, attitude, attire, and accent. English of the most pronounced and impressive type—but impressive upon as keen and thoroughbred an American observer as the famous New York detective chiefly because of the insipid and mildly obtrusive aristocracy that stuck out all over him.

He was tall and slender. He wore a suit of pronounced plaid. He was about twenty-three years old, with yellow hair and the fair skin of a straight-bred Anglo-Saxon. He wore a monocle with a cord dangling from it, and through which one watery blue eye glared larger and brighter than the other.

He had been hurrying up Fifth Avenue for about five minutes in a sort of subdued and desperate agitation, threading his way quite rudely through the stream of pedestrians always in that fashionable thoroughfare shortly before six on a pleasant October afternoon, and he incidentally had overtaken Nick Carter near the corner of Fifty-ninth Street.

He did not accost the detective because he knew him, or had the slightest idea of his vocation. It was purely by chance that he had appealed to the man he most needed. He obeyed a sudden, irrepressible impulse, that of one who scarce knew what else to do, when he grasped Nick's arm and stopped him, exclaiming apologetically:

"Oh, I say, old top!"

Nick sized him up with a glance. He saw more than others would have seen, that this stranger not only was deeply disturbed, but also in doubt what course to pursue. Nick merely said, nevertheless, tentatively:

"Well?"

The other responded with a forward thrust of his head, a more appealing scrutiny, and with native accent and characteristics that no attempt will be made to even suggest on paper.

"You'll pardon a chap, old top, won't you? I'm in a bally bad mess, so I am, and jolly well upset. Would you tell me where I could find an inspector—what your blooming people call a detective? I don't want any gumshoe bobbie, don't you know, but a ripping roarer who knows his beastly business and can keep his mouth closed. You see, old top—"

"What's the trouble, young man?" Nick interposed. "I may be able to aid you, or advise you. I am a detective—what your blooming English people call an inspector."

The subtle retort in the last was wasted upon his hearer. He gazed more sharply at Nick through his monocle, nevertheless, saying quickly:

"That's blasted lucky, then, don't you know? I can't account for it, 'pon my word, this running bunk against a man I wanted. What name, sir, may I ask?"

"My name is Nick Carter," replied the detective indifferently. "But what—"

"There it is again!" exclaimed the Englishman, interrupting with countenance lighting. "This is a blooming, blasted good wheeze. I've heard of you, sir. You're bally well known by name even in old Lunnon. I'm deuced well pleased, Mr. Carter, so I am."

He seemed to have temporarily forgotten his trouble, in his surprise and pleasure upon discovering the detective's identity. He even smiled and extended his hand, which was accepted and shaken in a perfunctory way.

Nick saw plainly, in fact, that the young man really was instinctively very frank and genuine, and that under his somewhat insipid and superficial personality he was possessed of true manly sentiments and probably some depth of character.

That he was a well-bred gentleman was equally manifest, moreover, and Nick was impelled to assist him, if possible. He brought him to the point at once, nevertheless, by replying:

"Granting all that, young man, what is your trouble? Why do you need a detective?"

"Because I'm blasted hard hit, don't you know?" he replied, serious again. "I've been jolly well robbed."

"Robbed of what?"

"My wife, sir."

"Robbed of your wife?" questioned Nick, surprised and almost inclined to laugh.

"That's the blooming truth, Mr. Carter, or how it looks to me. I'm as hard hit as if I'd got a jolly bash on the beak. She's a bally American girl, is Mollie, and—"

"Stop a moment," Nick interrupted again. "My time is valuable. I cannot listen to your digressions. Answer my questions briefly and to the point. I then may be able to aid you, if there is any real occasion."

"That's deuced kind, old top, on my word. If—"

"When did you lose your wife, and where?" Nick cut in a bit sharply.

"I didn't lose her. She was jolly well stolen; I'm sure of that."

"Where and when? By whom?"

"Blast it, how can I tell?" protested the Englishman, with wagging head. "We were walking down the avenue, Mollie and I, don't you know? A limousine shot by us, heading up-town. I heard it come to a blooming quick stop. A chauffeur came running back, a bally bounder in bottle-green livery. He tipped his lid, respectfullike, and said as how his fare had caught sight of Mollie when passing us and wanted to speak to her."

"His fare, eh? He was the driver of a taxicab, then?" put in Nick inquiringly.

"I reckon that's right, sir, but I won't be cock-sure."

"What more did he say?"

"Mollie asked the name of his fare, but he could not tell her. He said she had sent him to say a friend wanted to speak to her."

"His passenger was a woman, then?"

"I'm jolly well sure of that. I saw her hat and veil through the window."

"The taxicab must, then, have stopped quite near you," said Nick.

"A matter of thirty yards, sir, not more."

"Your wife went to see who was in the conveyance?"

"That's precisely what she did," nodded the Englishman. "Wait here, Archie, she said, and I'll return in a moment. I was jolly well surprised, don't you know, but what else could I do?"

"Nothing at all, perhaps."

"I always do what Mollie says. She hurried to the taxicab and stuck her head through the door. She shook hands with some one, too, as well as I could tell. Then the bally chauffeur shoved her into the car, or so it looked to me, and bounded to his seat and drove away at top speed. Dash it, what d'ye think of that?"

"What did you think of it?" Nick inquired.

"I was so beastly hard hit I couldn't think," cried the Englishman. "I chased after the bally cab as fast as possible, hoping it would stop and let Mollie down, but it sped out of sight into the park, and here I am. I'm deuced well convinced there's something wrong. Mollie wouldn't bolt off in that fashion. She's above serving me a scurvy trick. She—"

"One moment," Nick again interposed. "You feel quite sure, you say, that you saw the chauffeur force your wife into the cab?"

"It looked jolly well like it, Mr. Carter."

"Did you hear her speak, or utter a cry?"

"I did not, sir."

"Were there other persons near the taxicab at the time?"

"None nearer than I, sir, nor quite as near. I ran after it as fast as I could. I felt cock-sure, even then, it was a beastly job of some kind."

"Do you know of any reason for which your wife might be abducted?" Nick asked, more gravely.

"No, no reason at all, Mr. Carter. There can't be any reason."

"And you know of no person who might have designs upon her?"

"I do not," said the Englishman, with a groan at the mere suggestion. "What designs could one have? Mollie is my wife. She thinks the world of me. She's true-blue and deucedly clever and self-reliant. She—"

"Wait!" said Nick, checking him again. "You are English, I judge."

"Yes, of course."

"And your wife is an American girl?"

"She is, sir, and none better."

"Do you reside here in the city?"

"We are here only for a time. We are boarding in Fifty-third Street, near the avenue."

"Let's walk that way," said Nick. "It's barely possible that your wife will have been dropped at the boarding house before we reach it. How long before you appealed to me did this incident occur?"

"Not more than three or four minutes. We were about three blocks below here."

Nick remembered having seen a taxicab speeding up the avenue noticeably faster than usual at about that time. He had not observed it particularly, however, nor could he recall anything distinctive about it.

There were other reasons than that, moreover, for the interest he was taking in this stranger. He regarded the episode quite as seriously as the young Englishman himself. He knew much better than the other what daring and audacious crimes are committed in New York, and he began to suspect that this might be one of them.

Nick had decided to look at least a little deeper into the matter, therefore, and it was with that object in view that he suggested going to the Englishman's lodging house, which was only a few blocks south of where the two men had met.

Nick continued to question him while they walked briskly down the avenue.

"How long have you been in New York?" he inquired.

"I have been here only two weeks, Mr. Carter, this time," was the reply.

"Your second visit?"

"Yes. I was here about two months ago for the first time. I have been out in the bally Cripple Creek country to invest in some mines. Deucedly rough section, old top, with a beastly lot of bally bounders, but they dig out a jolly quantity of rich ore. 'Pon my word, I—"

"You are a man of means, then, I infer," put in Nick.

"Well, I have a bit of a fortune in my own name."

"By the way, speaking of that, what is your name?" Nick pointedly inquired.

The Englishman hesitated for half a second. Most men would not have noticed it. Nick was quick to detect it, suspecting deception, however, as well as some secret occasion for it.

"My name is Archie Waldron."

"Archie Waldron, eh?"

"Yes. I am English, you know, as you remarked, though I'm jolly well puzzled as to how you discovered it."

Nick did not inform him. Instead, as they turned into Fifty-third Street and approached the boarding house occupied by the Englishman, he inquired, more earnestly:

"Where had you been with your wife, or where were you going, Mr. Waldron, when this strange separation occurred?"

A tinge of red appeared in the Englishman's cheeks. He appeared somewhat embarrassed. He gazed at Nick for a moment, then said:

"We went out for a bit of a walk, Mr. Carter. It's deuced tiresome, you know, sitting around a bally boarding house. Here we are, too, and—"

"Wait one moment," Nick interrupted, as they arrived at the steps of the house. "I have something to say to you, Mr. Waldron."

"Glad of it, old top, on my word. What is it?"

"You already anticipate it," Nick replied impressively. "I can read that in your face. Now, young man, this matter may be even more serious than you really think. I have no idea that we shall find your wife here. There is no telling when she will return, by whom she was carried away, or how she can be traced and the truth discovered—unless you tell me the truth."

"But—"

"Your name is not Archie Waldron. You did not come out merely for a walk with your wife. You were going, or had been somewhere, with a definite object in view, and that possibly may have some bearing upon what followed."

"'Pon my word, sir—"

"Oh, there is nothing to it," Nick insisted. "I mean just what I say. You will be perfectly safe, Mr. Waldron, in frankly confiding in me. You must do so, too, or I shall drop this matter immediately. Under no other conditions will I enter this house."

# CHAPTER 2

## DOWN TO CASES

Nick Carter had a way of making himself felt under such circumstances. His impressive remarks were immediately effective. The Englishman turned even more pale and grave, gazing apprehensively at the detective, while he replied, with agitated voice:

"You're deucedly well right. I'd be a blooming idiot, Mr. Carter, if I couldn't see that. Come into the house, sir, and I'll tell you the whole beastly business. Your word is as good as a Bank of England note, sir, and I'll keep nothing from you."

"You have decided wisely," said Nick, while they mounted the steps. "In so far as the circumstances permit, I shall consider your disclosure strictly confidential."

"That's mighty kind, sir, and I'll pay you handsomely."

"Payment is an after-consideration. I will accept no more than my services warrant."

"You're deucedly clever, old top, and I'm proud to know you. Some jolly good fairy must have sent you my way in an hour of need. Come up to my room, sir."

The Englishman had opened the door with a latchkey, and he now led the way to an attractively furnished room on the second floor.

Among the first articles to catch Nick's eye, amid other evidence of feminine taste and sentiment, were two artistic photographs on the mantel. One was a likeness of his companion.

The other was that of a very beautiful girl still under twenty, a face that reflected culture and vivacity, and the winsome features and expression of which, with the finely poised head and shapely shoulders, might have been the ideal of a Raphael or Correggio.

Nick at once inferred rightly that this was the girl who apparently had been spirited away so boldly, as well as mysteriously, in so far as a motive had yet appeared.

The young Englishman looked disappointed when Nick's prediction was verified, his wife not being found there, and he at once waved the detective to a chair, saying with nervous haste and in his own peculiar fashion, which was much less frivolous than appears:

"You were jolly well right, Mr. Carter, and I'm confoundedly upset. What the devil can a poor chap do? I'm going to tell you all about it. How the dickens did you know, old top, that my name isn't Archie Waldron?"

"Because you hesitated when I questioned you," said Nick. "No man would shrink from stating his true name under such circumstances."

"Dash it! that was blasted clever, don't you know? I was a fall guy not to think of that. But you hit the bally nail on the nob. My name is not Waldron, 'pon my honor. I'm the fifth son of the Earl of Eggleston, and an only son by his second wife, the late Countess of Waldmere, from whom I got my title and a bally bit of a fortune. She died when I was born, and I became Lord Waldmere."

"I suspected something of the kind," Nick replied. "I find that I sized you up correctly."

"Did you really, now? Well, that's deuced kind and clever, 'pon my word. What's to be done, my dear fellow? We can't stay here, old top, while Mollie——"

"Now, Lord Waldmere, you're talking," Nick interrupted. "We must get down to rock-bottom as quickly as possible. You must leave me to determine what shall be done. I know more about New York and its deviltry than you could possibly imagine."

"That's jolly well right, sir, of course."

"All I require of you, Waldmere, is to tell me a straight story, as briefly as possible," Nick added familiarly. "What are you doing over here? Who was your American wife? Why are you living under an assumed name in a New York boarding house? Tell me all about it with as few words as possible."

Nick then obtained a straight story, in so far as the essential facts were concerned, but not without comments and digressions, from which Lord Waldmere appeared utterly unable to refrain, and which divested his story of anything like desirable brevity.

Briefly stated, however, it appeared that his young lordship, who in most respects was a worthy representative of one of the wealthy and most conservative families of the English aristocracy, had fallen deeply in love with a beautiful American chorus girl about three months before, who then was one of an American opera company singing in London.

In spite of the violent opposition and threats of his father, Lord Waldmere had married the girl, one Mary Royal, then only nineteen, but a girl of remarkable beauty and many accomplishments, and of unblemished and enviable reputation.

What followed was in line with the old, old story. His lordship was promptly disowned and disinherited. He at once left England and came to America with his bride, already having small interests in several Colorado mines, and bent upon investing in others a part of his personal fortune, which amounted to something like fifty thousand pounds, then tied up in English securities and mortgages.

Lord Waldmere had remained only ten days in New York after his arrival. He then went to Colorado with his wife to investigate various mining properties, concerning which he already was partly informed, and in which he anticipated investing quite heavily.

Lack of ready money, however, and his inability to realize immediately upon his home investments, had led him to take an unusual step, one taken upon the suggestion and advice of his wife, pending receipt of funds from a London agent.

Lord Waldmere had, in fact, raised ten thousand dollars by placing in pawn with the Imperial Loan Company his wife's valuable jewels, given to her before her marriage, and valued at about thirty thousand dollars. This not only had been done upon his wife's suggestion, but she also had made the deal and conducted the entire transaction, having had far more experience and being of a much more practical business mind than her husband himself. All of this money had since been invested in Colorado.

Returning to New a week before, Waldmere then communicated by cable with his London agent, who, during the interval, had converted some of his lordship's property into cash, and drafts were immediately sent him more than doubly sufficient to redeem the pledged jewels.

These funds had arrived that afternoon and were immediately placed on deposit. A little later Waldmere went with his wife to the office of the Imperial Loan Company to redeem the jewels, arriving there soon after five o'clock.

They were told, however, that the jewels were in a time-lock vault that had just been closed for the day, and which could not be opened until nine o'clock the following morning, when the jewels could be redeemed and the transaction ended.

This was perfectly satisfactory under the circumstances, of course, and Lady Waldmere promised to call with her husband the following morning. It was while they were returning to the boarding house, however, that they were separated in the extraordinary manner described.

Such was his lordship's story, told in his own peculiar way, and to which Nick Carter very attentively listened. It revealed the truth in so far as Waldmere could reveal it—but it by no means explained the disappearance of her ladyship, the beautiful American chorus girl for whom Waldmere had lost his heart and sacrificed his prestige.

Nick smiled somewhat significantly when the Englishman had finished. He glanced at the photograph on the mantel, remarking agreeably:

"Well, well, Waldmere, you were hard hit indeed by the pretty American girl. In view of the incentive to many of our international marriages, your conduct is really quite refreshing. I rather like you for it. That is a photograph of Lady Waldmere, I infer."

"Yes, taken in London," bowed Waldmere, evidently deeply pleased with the detective's comments.

"A very beautiful woman, indeed."

"She jolly well is, Mr. Carter, and worthy of—"

"Of all your devotion, Waldmere, no doubt," Nick familiarly interrupted. "But we must not drift away from the matter. We must get onto our job and stick to it, or valuable time may be lost."

"I agree with you."

"None of the circumstances you have stated seem to present, on the surface at least, any reasonable explanation of what has occurred, nor any consistent motive for felonious designs upon her," Nick added. "Unless she soon returns, nevertheless, there can be no doubt that she is a victim of knavery of some kind, that does not appear on the surface. Let me ask you a few questions. I then may hit upon some theory to fit the case."

"That's a ripping good idea, old top," Lord Waldmere nodded. "Come on with them."

"To begin with, then, has your wife many acquaintances here in town?"

"Hardly any, sir, 'pon my word. She is a Kentucky girl, and has spent but little time in this bally city. We have met none during either of our visits. We live very privately."

"It is quite improbable, then, that the occupant of the taxi-cab was a friend, or even an acquaintance," Nick pointed out. "Deception having been employed, therefore, we must assume that she was forcibly carried away. That also appears in the fact that you think the driver thrust her into the cab."

"I'm deuced well sure of that, Mr. Carter," Waldmere again declared. "The bally bounder placed his hand squarely on her shoulder, sir, and gave her a push. I can almost swear to that. If she—"

"Let me do most of the talking, Waldmere," Nick interrupted. "I wish to get at the salient points as quickly as possible. Answer me with merely an affirmative, or negative, when you can."

"Very well, sir."

"Has your father, or any of your family, ever threatened the girl because of your marriage?" Nick then inquired. "In other words, Waldmere, do you believe any of them capable of a conspiracy against her?"

"No, sir," protested the Englishman quickly. "They are above anything of that kind. Besides, Mr. Carter, they have jolly well cast us both out. No one knows where to find us."

"You think, then, that they may be safely eliminated from any connection with this affair?"

"Yes, absolutely."

"We must seek nearer home, then, for a motive," said Nick. "Had Miss Royal any former admirer who might—"

"No, no; nothing of the kind." Lord Waldmere quickly shook his head. "Her sweet heart has been an open book for me to read at will. There is nothing in that, sir."

"And you recall no incentive, or circumstance, that might have a bearing upon this matter?"

"No, none, Mr. Carter."

"Let's consider, then, the one nearest to it—your visit to the Imperial Loan Company," said Nick. "I think you said that Lady Waldmere did most of the business."

"She did the whole blooming business," Lord Waldmere quickly assured him. "She's jolly well fitted for it, is Mollie, while I'm a doughhead and—"

"I understand," Nick cut in. "You went with her to redeem the jewels, which had been pledged for ten thousand dollars. Did she have the money on her person? That may have been the incentive for the crime, if such it turns out to be."

"But that can't be, don't you know?" Waldmere at once protested. "Mollie had the bally ticket for the pledge, but she had no money. I had a certified bank check for the amount. Here it is, sir. See for yourself."

Nick merely glanced at the check, which Lord Waldmere hastily drew from his pocketbook. It bore the current date and corroborated the Englishman's statements.

"It seems to knock that theory on the head," Nick said thoughtfully, after a moment. "Nevertheless, by Jove, it may be that the jewels—"

Nick broke off abruptly, not stating what he had in mind. Instead, drawing forward in his chair, he said, more earnestly:

"By the way, Lord Waldmere, did your wife transact this business under her own name, or a fictitious one?"

"An assumed name, of course."

"The one by which you are known here?"

"No. She used another."

"What was it?"

Lord Waldmere scratched his head, staring desperately at the carpet for several moments.

"Dash it, sir! I've jolly well forgotten," he cried dubiously. "'Pon my honor, Mr. Carter, I can't remember."

"Rack your brains for a moment," Nick suggested, though he had no great hope of any desirable result.

"Hang it, sir! I'm giving them a ripping racking. But Mollie always kept the bally ticket, you see, and I had no hand in the blooming business. She has a head for it, don't you know, and I always let her run things for me. Blast it, sir, I can't remember!"

"Well, well, never mind," Nick said, a bit bluntly. "Whom did you see in the loan office?"

"The jolly manager, I think."

"Do you remember his name?"

"'Pon my word, sir, I don't," said Waldmere, with a groan over his inability to be of any material aid. "I don't know that I heard his bally name, sir, as far as that goes. Molly did all of the talking."

"What was said, or done?"

"Very little, sir, 'pon my word. Mollie turned in the ticket to a dinky clerk in a window. He took it to a back room, as I remember, and in about five minutes the bally manager came out."

"What did he say?" Nick inquired.

"He said as how the jewels were in the vault, which had been closed about five o'clock for the day, and that it couldn't be opened until to-morrow morning."

"He stated that it had a time lock, didn't he?"

"Exactly. That's just what he said."

"And that your wife could redeem the jewels if she were to call to-morrow morning?"

"Precisely," Lord Waldmere nodded. "That's all there was to the blooming business."

Nick did not feel so sure of it. He saw plainly, however, that there was nothing more to be learned from the titled Englishman, who obviously knew as little of business as a lad in knickerbockers.

More than an hour had passed since the episode on the avenue. There was no indication of Lady Waldmere's return, nor did Nick really expect it. He glanced at his watch and found that it was nearly seven o'clock.

"Dash it! I'm deucedly upset," Waldmere remarked, and he really looked so. "What the dickens am I to do? What—"

Nick interrupted him kindly, but impressively.

"There is only one wise thing for you to do, Lord Waldmere," said he. "You must leave this matter to me and do precisely what I direct. If your wife has been abducted, or is a victim of other knavery, I will leave no stone unturned to find her and punish the crooks. I can accomplish both, perhaps, while you would surely fail."

"You're jolly well right, Mr. Carter, as far as that goes," Waldmere frankly admitted.

"You must see, then, that my advice is sound," said Nick. "I will take the case, if you wish, but you must promise to follow my instructions."

"That's deucedly kind, sir, and I'll do so. I will, sir, 'pon my honor."

"Very good," said Nick. Give the matter no publicity, then, at present. Remain here quietly until to-morrow morning, stating to others in the house merely that your wife is away for a short time. I don't want the matter to reach the newspapers."

"Dear me, no!"

"Be silent, then, and discreet. Here is a card with my address and telephone number. Is there a telephone in this house?"

"There is, sir," Waldmere nodded.

"If your wife returns before morning, then, call up my office and inform whomever answers you," Nick directed. "That would probably end the matter. If she does not return, however, which now seems more probable, you may expect me here at half past eight to-morrow morning. I then will begin a thorough investigation. In other words, Lord Waldmere, I'm going at this like a bull at a gate."

The last was added chiefly to encourage the down-hearted Englishman, who, strange to say, appeared to detect it. For he pulled himself together with a manly effort, then adjusted his monocle to gaze more intently at the detective, whose hand he warmly grasped with both of his.

"'Pon my honor, old top, I can't find words to thank you," he said gratefully. "I really can't, don't you know."

"Don't try, Lord Waldmere," Nick replied, pressing his hand. "Merely do only what I have directed. Keep a stiff upper lip and leave this matter to me. I'll call the turn, all right, as sure as you're a foot high."

# CHAPTER 3

## HOW NICK SIZED IT UP

Nick Carter came out from dinner in his Madison Avenue residence after eight o'clock, two hours later than usual. Instead of going to his business office, he entered his private library, saying to Joseph, his butler, as he passed him in the deep, attractively furnished hall:

"Send Chick and Patsy to me. They're in the office."

Nick had waited only a few moments, when he was joined by his chief assistant, Chick Carter, who was presently followed by Patsy Garvan. Both knew that something of importance was in the wind, and Nick at once proceeded to tell them of what it consisted, covering all of the essential points of the case.

"Gee, that's some puzzle, chief, for fair!" commented Patsy, after listening attentively. "What's the game? His royal nob from England must be a decent sort of a chap, after all, don't you know. He sure has been dead square with the chorus girl."

"So he is, Patsy, and less shallow than he appears," Nick replied. "But he don't know enough about business to last him overnight. Evidently, however, his wife is a keen and clever girl, as well as handsome."

"Why not? She's an American girl," said Patsy.

"That's one reason why I took on the case," smiled Nick.

"The Imperial Loan Company," put in Chick. "Why, I know that concern. It's nothing else but a high-grade pawnshop. It was established by Isaac Meyer several years ago. I knew him when he had a shop in the Bowery. But he's nearly down and out, now with creeping paralysis. He never leaves home."

"Where is that?" Nick inquired.

"Over in Columbus Avenue."

"Who runs his business?"

"His manager," said Chick. "A man named Morris Garland. He has been with Meyer since he opened the Fifth Avenue place. It's only a few blocks from where you met the Englishman."

"I know the place very well, Chick, but none of the inmates," said Nick. "What do you know about Garland?"

"He's all aboveboard, Nick, as far as I know," Chick replied. "There is only one out about him, if that really cuts any ice."

"What is that?"

"I have seen him quite frequently with Stuart Floyd. They appear to be very friendly. You know Floyd, of course. He's about as keen and slick a fellow as can be found in this old town."

"Do you think so?"

"Don't you?"

"I don't know much about him, Chick, save that he is a well-known man about town. The police have nothing on him, have they?"

"No, nothing that I know of," Chick admitted. "Floyd has no record, to be sure, barring a record that makes him a mystery to me, at least."

"Why a mystery?"

"Because he has no visible means of support, yet he always has plenty of money, or appears to have," said Chick.

"He inherited nothing, nevertheless, for I knew his people, as I have known him for years."

"I see."

"He has lived by his wits since he was fifteen. I never knew him to do a stroke of work. At thirty, nevertheless," Chick pointed out, "he frequents the best hotels and restaurants, lives like a lord, dresses like a millionaire, and spends money more lavishly than most of them. He apparently is a thoroughbred sport and man about town. But where does the coin come from? How does he get by? If that don't constitute a mystery, Nick, what the dickens does? I'm from Missouri. You'll have to show me."

Nick laughed.

"We are drifting from the more important matter," said he. "You know of nothing wrong in his relations with Morris Garland, do you?"

"No, nothing," Chick allowed. "I've told you all I know about him."

"He is not alone in those respects," Nick replied. "There are hundreds like him. I have heard, of course, that Stuart Floyd is a slick fellow. He really looks it, as far as that goes, for he is as clean-cut, attractive a man as one often meets. That's neither here nor there, however, at this stage of the game. We'll get back to Hecuba."

"Do you suspect the Imperial Loan Company, chief, in connection with Lady Waldmere's disappearance?" asked Patsy.

"I do."

"Why?"

"For two reasons," said Nick. "First, because there seems to be no one else to suspect. Second, because the episode occurred so soon after her visit to the loan company. That suggests a possible connection between them."

"I see the point."

"Furthermore, there are ten thousand dollars involved, or jewels valued at close upon thirty," Nick added. "Those may be the incentive to knavery of some kind. There seems to be no other motive for a crime, in fact, assuming that a crime really has been committed."

"That's right, too, chief," nodded Patsy. "There seems to be nothing else to be gained, if Lord Waldmere had told a straight story."

"I have no doubt of that."

"But what could the loan company gain by abducting the woman?" Chick questioned, perplexed. "The jewels must be in their possession."

"Very true," Nick admitted. "They knew that Lady Waldmere had called to redeem them, and that she must have brought the funds with which to do so. They may not have known, however, that she intended redeeming the pledge with a certified check. They may have thought that she had the ten thousand dollars in cash on her person."

"Gee! that listens good to me, chief!" cried Patsy, quick to see the point. "That seems to be the only way to size it up."

"That is one way, at least," Nick replied, smiling a bit oddly.

"But it must have been a mighty slick job, Nick, in that case," Chick objected, with manifest doubt of the theory advanced by the other.

"It was a slick job."

"But how could they have framed it up so quickly?"

"What are you driving at?" Patsy demanded, turning upon Chick. "Why quickly?"

"That ought to be plain enough even to you," Chick retorted. "Lord Waldmere stated that he and his wife were in the office of the loan company only about five minutes."

"Well, I admit that."

"It is obvious, too, that their visit could not have been anticipated," Chick proceeded to argue. "Neither Morris Garland, nor the assistant manager, Moses Hart, could have known that Lady Waldmere had any intention of redeeming the jewelry at just that time."

"True again, old man," nodded Patsy, with an expression of perplexity returning to his face.

"That's what I mean, then, by their having framed up the job so quickly," Chick forcibly added.

"I get you."

"They would have had only five minutes in which to have laid their plans and made all the arrangements for executing them. That's a mighty short time in which to shape up such a job, to say nothing of getting ready to carry it out. It's not a simple stunt to pick up a woman on Fifth Avenue and get away with her from under her husband's eyes."

"Say, you're getting wiser every minute, Chick," cried Patsy, laughing. "I begin to think there really is something in what you say."

"You ought to have seen it before."

"What do you say, chief?"

Nick laughed and knocked the ashes from the cigar he was smoking.

"Chick's argument is all right, Patsy, as far as it goes," he replied. "We know that the couple were only a short time in the office of the loan company, and that their visit could not have been anticipated. We are not pinned down to five minutes, however."

"What do you mean?" questioned Chick.

"What Lord Waldmere really said was this—that, after talking with one of the clerks, who very likely was the assistant manager, the latter went into Garland's private office, where he remained about five minutes before either of them came out to resume the discussion."

"Gee! that's right, too," nodded Patsy.

"And it is quite significant," Nick added. "It certainly would not have taken Hart five minutes to state merely what the couple wanted."

"Surely not."

"Garland could have come out and joined them in half a minute, as far as that goes. Why, then, did he not do so? What were the two men doing that occupied five full minutes? It looks very much to me as if they were framing a job."

"But—"

"One moment, Chick," Nick interposed. "I know you're going to object again to my theory. I advanced that, however, as a matter of fact, only to point out that there could have been a reasonable motive for knavery."

"Ah, that's different," said Chick, smiling.

"I have no idea, nevertheless, assuming that Garland and Hart are back of this business, that they aimed to rob Lady Waldmere of money supposed to be on her person," Nick continued. "They would not have acted upon a mere supposition. They first would have made absolutely sure that she had the money."

"Certainly," Chick nodded. "That goes without saying."

"All the same, chief, there was a job framed up for some reason during those five minutes," Patsy said roundly. "I'd wager my bankroll on that."

"I think so, too," Nick agreed.

"But what's the game?" Chick questioned, still doubtful.

"Can't you think of one that may have been necessary?"

"Not on the spur of the moment."

"I can," said Nick, smiling.

"Well, well, out with it," laughed Chick, coloring slightly. "What do you suspect?"

Nick laid aside his cigar.

"Pull up a little nearer," said he. "I can tell you with very few words what I suspect—and how we may contrive to clinch my suspicions."

# CHAPTER 4

## NICK DECLARES HIMSELF

Nick Carter's anticipation proved to be correct. He received no telephone communication from Lord Waldmere, informing him that his pretty American wife had returned. In accord with his promise to the Englishman, therefore, while Chick and Patsy prepared to carry out the instructions given them, Nick appeared at the boarding house in Fifty-third Street at precisely half past eight that morning and rang the bell.

As the saying goes, however, Nick's own mother would not have recognized him. He was clad in a rather obtrusive plaid suit of pronounced English cut. He looked portly and imposing. He carried a heavy ebony cane. His strong, clean-cut face was artfully disguised. He could have walked through the Strand or Piccadilly, and readily have been taken for a Bond Street banker on his way to business.

Nick directed the servant to inform Mr. Waldron that the friend he was expecting had arrived, and the detective was presently conducted to the first-floor front, which he entered and closed the door.

Lord Waldmere, looking white and haggard after a sleepless night, stared at him in blank amazement.

"Oh, I say!" he exclaimed. "There is some beastly mistake. I'm not expecting—"

"Yes, you are, Waldmere," Nick interrupted, smiling and speaking in his customary tones. "There is no mistake. I told you, you know, that I was going at this case like a bull at a gate."

Waldmere's face lighted wondrously.

"Oh, by Jove!" he cried, hand extended. "You are—"

"The man you expect," Nick interposed, more seriously. "Don't be surprised at seeing me thus disguised. My face is very well known to the denizens of the underworld, and I frequently must get in my work under cover."

"You are jolly well covered, sir, as to that," Waldmere replied, smiling significantly. "I'd never know you. I'd take you for some blooming banker, or—"

"That is precisely what I aimed at," Nick replied. "But we have no time to waste. You have heard nothing from your wife, of course?"

"Not a word, or—"

"Or you would have advised me, certainly," Nick cut in again. "We will get right at this matter, then. Sit down while I give you a few instructions."

Lord Waldmere complied, all attention.

Half an hour later, or about quarter past nine, a taxicab stopped in front of the quarters of the Imperial Loan Company, which Nick and his companion entered, or that part of the establishment open to its patrons.

There was an atmosphere of dignity and business solidarity in the place. A long counter with a high brass lattice divided the public room. Back of it were two clerks and the assistant manager, Moses Hart, the former talking in whispers to customers through narrow windows. Three large steel safes and a vault in one of the walls had an imposing appearance. Off to the right were two private rooms, accessible only through the latticed inclosure. The doors of both were partly open.

There were half a dozen customers engaged at the windows, or waiting their turn, when Nick and Waldmere entered.

One among them was a seedily clad man with a sallow countenance and a scraggly brown beard, who appeared decidedly down in the world. A rusty derby hat was pulled nearly down to his ears. He was waiting to pawn a bit of jewelry, and a certain shifty light in his restless eyes denoted that he awaited the transaction with some misgivings, indicating that where he had obtained the bauble might consistently be questioned. He glanced suspiciously at Nick and the Englishman, then turned his head, as if to avoid observation.

Nick paid no attention to the fellow, however, but at once approached a window at one end of the long counter and nearer the private office, Lord Waldmere following at his elbow.

Moses Hart came to meet them at the window, a short dark man of forty, with gold-bowed spectacles astride his somewhat prominent nose.

"Good morning, gentlemen," said he, rubbing his hands and leaning over the counter. "What can I do for you this morning?"

Nick already had directed Waldmere to let him do all of the talking.

"Are you the manager here?" he inquired.

"The assistant manager," Hart corrected, smiling and bowing obsequiously. "What is your business?"

"We wish to redeem some valuable jewels which you are holding as collateral," said Nick. "You loaned my friend, here, ten thousand dollars on them, which he now is ready to pay, with the accrued interest. He called yesterday afternoon with his wife, who—"

"Dear me!" Hart quietly exclaimed, interrupting. "Yes, yes, I remember that one of the clerks mentioned it. Unfortunately, the vault containing the jewels had been closed for the day and could not be opened. Let me have our ticket, or voucher, given you for the pledge and I will get them."

Nick had had a constant eye on Hart's face. He saw that the man lost color, that an apprehensive expression in his squinted eyes evinced a perturbation that he could not entirely conceal. This convinced Nick that he was on the right track, though he realized that he still was laboring under some difficulties.

"Unfortunately, too, we are not in possession of the ticket for the loan," he replied. "It is in the keeping of his wife, who has gone away for a time with a friend."

"You must communicate with her, then, and have her send you the ticket," Hart rejoined.

"We cannot do that."

"Not do it?"

"No. We are not informed of her address."

"But you cannot expect us to redeem the pledge to any person except the holder of the ticket," Hart quickly protested. "That is the only safeguard for both parties. You must bring the ticket, of course, in order to obtain the jewels. Otherwise, we cannot possibly let you have them."

"But—"

"Oh, there is nothing to it," Hart insisted. "We do business in no other way."

"See here!" Nick exclaimed, and his voice took on a somewhat threatening ring. "Unless you—"

"One moment, sir," Hart again interrupted. "I will speak to our manager, Mr. Garland. He will talk with you. Wait just one moment."

Hart vanished from the window, and through the brass lattice Nick saw him hasten into one of the private offices.

Five minutes passed and he did not reappear.

"This looks deucedly like not getting them, by Jove," whispered Waldmere, gazing dubiously at the detective.

"I don't expect to get them," Nick muttered.

"No?"

"I came here only to size up these fellows and hear what they would say," Nick quietly added. "Say nothing while I am talking with the manager, if he ever decides to show up."

"You think—"

"There's nothing to it. The two men are discussing the situation. They don't like it for some reason. I must find later of what that reason consists. It may be the key to the whole business."

"I'm jolly well convinced that—"

"Quiet. Here comes the manager."

A tall, somewhat cadaverous man of forty was approaching from the private office. His bushy brows were knit, and he had an aggressive aspect that gave promise of nothing favorable. He came straight to the window at which Nick and Waldmere were standing.

"Are you the gentlemen who wish to redeem some jewels?" he asked abruptly.

"Yes," said Nick shortly.

"I am Mr. Garland, the manager. My assistant has told me what you have said. There really is nothing we can do for you. You will have to bring the ticket for the pledge in order to redeem it."

"But we cannot get the ticket until this gentleman's wife returns," Nick replied.

"Where has she gone?"

"We don't know. She is away with a friend."

"Is the ticket in her name?"

"Yes."

"What name?"

"We don't know that, either," said Nick. "She used a fictious name when she negotiated the loan."

"Why did she do that?" Garland demanded. "There should have been no occasion for it. We do all of our business aboveboard and expect no less of our patrons. Really, gentlemen, this matter don't look quite right to me. You will have to wait until the woman returns, or sends you the ticket."

Nick Carter's disguised face took on a more threatening frown. He pressed nearer the window, replying, in peppery tones:

"This don't look right to you, eh? What is it, sir, that don't look right to you."

"We will not discuss that point," said Garland curtly. "I have told you the only way by which you can redeem the pledge and obtain the jewels."

"No, you haven't," snapped Nick hotly. "I can appeal to the authorities. I can call in the police. I'll do it, too, unless you come down from your high horse."

"Don't be foolish, my man," said Garland, frowning.

"I'm not at all sure that the jewels are here. I'll find out— I'll make it a point to find out."

"Nonsense! You talk like an ass," Garland protested.

"Produce them, then," frothed Nick. "Let's have a look at them, at least. If they—"

"They are in the time-lock vault, with a thousand other pledges," Garland hurriedly explained. "I cannot produce them without searching the entire vault. You cannot tell me the name under which they are pledged. I have no other means of finding them immediately. It would take me half a day to go through the vault and identify them. You talk like a fool, sir. Bring the ticket and the amount of the loan, and you shall have the jewels within half a minute."

Nick continued to storm and argue.

While this was in progress, attracting the attention of all in the place, Moses Hart came from the private office. He did not pause to join in the dissension, however, but at once went on to a narrow window at the lower end of the long counter—that at which the seedy, sinister-looking man then was waiting.

Bending close to the window, Hart winked significantly and said, with his voice lowered:

"Do you want to make a bit of money?"

The fellow's shifty eyes lighted eagerly.

"Does a hungry cat want meat?" he returned, in an expressive whisper.

"What's your name?" Hart asked.

"Jerry Nolan."

"I want to find out who that man is who—"

"The gink doing the talking?"

"Yes."

"I get you, boss."

"I want you to follow him when he leaves here, and find out," Hart went on. "Pick both of them up when they leave."

"I'll do it, boss! I'll find out for you, or break a leg," Nolan earnestly assured him.

"Don't return here to tell me, however," Hart added. "I want you to inform my partner."

"The geeser having the spiel with the hothead?"

"Yes. I will tell you where you must meet him."

"Come over with it," nodded Nolan.

Hart hastily informed him.

"I get you, boss," Nolan repeated. "I'm on to the job, and will be there, all right."

"Make sure you're not detected," Hart cautioned.

"Leave me alone for that."

"And say nothing about this."

"And for that, too," whispered Nolan, with an expressive leer.

"That's all, then. Go ahead."

Nolan turned away from the window. He bestowed another swift, furtive glance upon the detective, then hitched up his baggy trousers and sneaked out of the place.

Nick Carter, after an apparently vain mission, departed with Lord Waldmere five minutes later.

# CHAPTER V

## NOLAN MAKES A DISCOVERY

Jerry Nolan proved as good as his word, in so far as what he had been directed to accomplish was concerned.

He followed Nick Carter and Lord Waldmere from the quarters of the loan company, and something like an hour following their departure after their apparently vain mission, Nolan put in an appearance in the upper section of Amsterdam Avenue, where he had been directed to await the coming of Mr. Morris Garland.

If one were to have judged from the expression on Nolan's sinister face, however, one would have felt reasonably sure that he could not be wisely trusted, that he had sized up the circumstances from his own evil standpoint, and was bent upon taking further advantage of them than he seemed likely to derive. In other words, Nolan appeared to suspect that there was something crooked in the wind, and was resolved to make the most of it.

All this would have been even more obvious to an observer of Nolan's actions upon approaching the appointed rendezvous.

He did not wait on the corner, as he had been directed. Instead, he slunk around it, apparently watching the pedestrians within his range of vision in the avenue, and presently he stole over to an opposite doorway, which seemed to afford a more desirable vantage point, and from which he continued his sinister vigil.

Presently he sighted among the comparatively few people then in that part of the avenue the man he was expecting. He recognized him at once, though he then was nearly a block away and on the opposite side of the thoroughfare.

There could be no mistaking the tall figure and dark, cadaverous face of the head manager of the Imperial Loan Company.

Nolan's eyes lighted when Garland appeared in the near distance. One would have said that he was thinking of the reward for the scurrilous work he had agreed to do.

"Here's where I'll get mine, all right," he said to himself. "I'll make him settle sooner or later. I reckon I'd better hike over to the corner where I'm to meet him, or he might suspect that I—"

Nolan's train of thought was brought to an abrupt end by a sudden, unexpected move of the other.

Morris Garland turned from the sidewalk and quickly crossed the avenue. He then walked quite slowly, with his gaze directed to the side from which he had come, and once he paused for a moment to gaze at the door and windows of an opposite house, one of a long brick block.

Nolan took a look at it, also, but he could discover nothing warranting Garland's manifest interest in the house.

The door was closed. The curtains at most of the windows were drawn down. Some of the windows were dusty, and the front steps had not recently been swept. The house looked, in fact, aside from its furnishings, as if it was unoccupied.

"What's hit him, now?" Nolan asked himself. "Why is he sizing up that crib? Nobody home but the gas, and that's leaking out. I wonder—"

Another move by Garland broke Nolan's train of thought.

Garland quickly recrossed the avenue, then hastened up to the appointed corner, glancing sharply in all directions.

"Looking for me," Nolan tersely thought, slinking back in the doorway. "I'll let him look for half a minute and see what he'll do next."

Garland did not look as long as half a minute. He evidently assumed that Nolan had not yet completed his work and arrived there. He turned abruptly and hastened to a house on the opposite corner of the cross-street, entering with a key.

"That must be where the bloke lives," Nolan reasoned. "That's why I was told to come up here to report. I'll see— huh! there he is again."

Nolan caught sight of him at one of the front windows. He could see his dark face between the lace draperies. He watched it intently, with even a more sinister look in his own keen eyes.

Garland evidently was watching for the expected man.

"I'll sneak out when he isn't watching, and then show up on the corner," Nolan said to himself. "He won't be wise, then, to the fact that I got here first. I'll put something over on him, all right, or I've doped out this business all wrong."

Something like five minutes later, after waiting for a favorable opportunity, Nolan appeared on the street corner opposite Garland's residence. He had been waiting only a moment when the latter emerged from the house and hastened over to join him.

"Well, you're here, Nolan, at last," he said, a bit curtly.

"Sure I'm here, boss," Nolan nodded. "You can always bank on my making good."

"Have you done what Hart directed?"

"The geeser who hired me? Yes, of course. I sure have done it. If I hadn't, I wouldn't be here," said Nolan, with an expressive leer.

"Well, what did you learn?" Garland demanded, more sharply eying him.

"I followed the two blokes down Fifth Avenue about three blocks, but I couldn't get next to anything they were saying," Nolan proceeded to report. "They parted on a corner, and then I followed the big guy, him as put the peppery spiel in the pawnshop."

"Where did he go?"

"Over to a house in Madison Avenue."

"Did you find out his name?"

"Sure I did," Nolan declared, much as if such a question was needless. "Trust me for that. I was wise to it, all right, when I piped him going in that crib."

"Who is he? What do you know about him?"

"He's a fly gun, boss; that's what he is. He's the biggest squeeze in the whole dick outfit. His name is Carter."

"Not Nick Carter?"

"That's what."

"Are you sure of it, absolutely sure of it?"

"As sure as if a house fell on me," Nolan forcibly asserted. "Why wouldn't I be? I've had him after me more'n once. He was made up with grease paint and spinach, all right, but I was wise to his true mug when he went up the steps and into the house. I knew before where the dick lived. What's the game, boss? I could help you further, if you fancied putting me wise."

Garland's dark face had, upon learning the name of Waldmere's companion that morning, taken on a look of more serious concern. It vanished almost instantly, however, and his teeth met with a vicious snap, smacking defiance, which evidently impelled Nolan to venture offering his further assistance.

Garland received the suggestion with a darker frown, however, and quickly shook his head.

"There isn't any game, my man," he said, quite sternly. "You put that idea out of your head, and keep it out. You were not employed for this work because of any game, but because we had no one else whom we could send conveniently at that time."

"Beg pardon, boss," Nolan quickly responded. "I'm wise, all right, now that you've put me next. It was the two coveys, Carter and the other gink, whom you think were playing some kind of a game."

"That's just the size of it," Garland hastened to assure him.

"I'm wise, all right, boss, now that you've told me."

"Both men were strangers to me," Garland added, in an explanatory way. "We suspected them of trickery and wanted to learn who they were, or more particularly the one you say is Nick Carter."

"You can bank on that, boss."

"It's all right, then, no doubt, for Nick Carter would not have engaged in any crooked work," Garland proceeded. "He must have had some other object in view. I shall probably be informed sooner or later. What do I owe you for your services?"

"That's up to you, boss," said Nolan, apparently content to drop the matter and accept what was offered, as well as the explanation just made.

"Will a ten-dollar note pay you?" questioned Garland, taking out a roll of money.

"Sure thing, boss, and then some."

"Let it keep your mouth closed, also," Garland added, stripping off a bank note from the roll. "I wouldn't want Carter to think I have any reason to have suspected him."

"I'm dumb," Nolan assured him, eagerly accepting the money.

"You will say nothing about it, eh?"

"On my word."

"Not even if—"

"Forget it!" Nolan cut in pointedly. "Forget it, boss; I have."

"Very good," Garland said approvingly. "See that you don't recall it."

He turned away with the last, quickly crossing the street and entering his residence. From one of the windows, however, he proceeded to watch Nolan down the avenue, until the seedy, sinister fellow vanished around a distant corner.

But Mr. Jerry Nolan was nothing if not crafty. He did not so much as glance back before turning the corner. Nor did he then pay further attention to Garland to see whether he left his house.

As he was passing that at which the pawnbroker had paused to gaze, however, Nolan glanced furtively at the door. He saw there was no name plate on it. He saw the dust on the steps and the soiled windows on the second floor, and he came to a perfectly natural conclusion.

"There's been something doing in this crib, or that Pawnee Indian would not have had so much interest in it," he said to himself. "It appears to be unoccupied. I'll nose around a bit and make sure of it. Then I'll find out whether there's only ten bucks for me in this job."

Nolan fixed in his mind the precise location of the house by counting from the end of the block. He then walked around to the next street, from which he stealthily picked his way through an alley until he could see the back of the suspected dwelling.

It would have confirmed the suspicions of any discerning man. The drawn curtains, the soiled windows, the closed shutters of those in the rear yard—all denoted that the house, though furnished, had not been recently occupied, unless for some covert purpose.

Nolan promptly came to another conclusion—that he would sneak into the house and see what more he could learn.

He went about it with the skill and caution of a professional sneak thief, which he looked more like than anything else. He crept through the alley and into the yard back of the house, where he crouched briefly under the high board fence to study the back windows of all the near dwellings.

Feeling sure that he had not been seen, he then took several skeleton keys from his pocket, quickly selecting one which he thought would serve his purpose.

It did.

Within half a minute Nolan had quietly unlocked the rear door and stepped noiselessly into a back basement hall, closing the door after him.

There he waited and listened, scarce breathing, until five full minutes had passed.

Not a sound came from any part of the house.

Not a sign of life could be seen in the dusty, dimly lighted hall.

Nolan then crept up the narrow stairway, still listening and alert.

There seemed to be, however, no occasion for such exquisite caution. Nolan reached the next floor, that on the level with the front street. He peered into one room after another, but discovered nothing wrong.

The kitchen looked cold and out of commission. The shutters were closed. The range and iron sink were smeared with vaseline to prevent rusting. Dust had collected on them, and they looked gray and dirty.

The dining room was uninviting. The sideboard was destitute, the polished table bare. The library, sitting room, and parlor, all were in order, but dim, cheerless, and deserted.

Nolan crept up to the next floor.

He peered into two front chambers, both neatly furnished, but he saw nothing of special interest.

He then stole toward the rear of the house.

He came to the open door of an interior room, one having no window. It was lighted only from the hall, save the artificial light, then switched off.

Nolan stopped and peered into this dim bedroom. Something on the unopened bed caught his eye—and Nolan involuntarily caught his breath.

He beheld a motionless figure, clad in a dark-blue suit, with shapely white hands crossed on its breast, with upturned, hueless face, as colorless as if death had lately claimed her—the face and figure of a surpassingly beautiful woman.

# CHAPTER 6

## HOW IT WAS DONE

Jerry Nolan was not rattled by the discovery he had made. It was not in his nature to be upset by anything short of a cyclone or an earthquake.

He gazed in for several moments at the motionless form on the bed, then tiptoed into the room to make a closer inspection.

"Is she dead?" he asked himself. "Has she been croaked by crooks?"

Nolan paused beside the bed, bending above her.

It seemed to him that he had never beheld a more beautiful face.

He touched her hand and found it cold, then listened and looked in vain for any sign that she was breathing.

There was an ugly gleam in Nolan's eyes when he straightened up and turned toward the door. He caught sight of a switch key on the wall, and realized that with more light he could better determine the woman's condition. He turned the key and a flood of electric light filled the room.

When he swung round again other objects met Nolan's gaze. The woman's hat and jacket were lying on a chair. Beside them lay an open hand bag. It contained only a dainty lace handkerchief. Her purse and other valuables evidently had been stolen.

Her kid gloves had been tossed upon a bureau. Near them on the bureau, placed in a small china tray, was a slender object, that glistened brightly in the electric light.

Nolan approached and gazed at it.

It was a small glass hypodermic syringe, nearly filled with a colorless fluid.

A scrap of paper, on which a few words were typewritten, had been placed under the tray.

Nolan drew it out and read:

"This woman is only drugged. Inject the contents of the syringe into her arm to revive her."

Nolan did not hesitate.

He took up the syringe with the familiarity of a physician, or of a dope fiend accustomed to using one, and again approached the bed.

Drawing up the sleeve from the woman's shapely arm, he plunged the needle through the fair skin and injected the contents of the syringe, which he then replaced on the bureau.

Nolan then put a chair near the side of the bed and sat down to await the result of this treatment.

He had not long to wait.

Scarce five minutes had passed when a tinge of color appeared in the woman's pale cheeks.

Her lips parted slightly and Nolan then could detect that she was breathing. Another minute brought a deep-drawn sigh and a low moan, soon followed by a fluttering of her eyelids.

"She's still in the ring, all right," Nolan congratulated himself. "They were a clever bunch, for fair, that did this job. Ten bucks, eh? I'll soon see about that ten bucks' gag. They'll come down handsomely for this, those two rats. Ah, now her lamps are lighted!"

The woman had opened her eyes.

She stared up at Nolan vacantly for several moments, too dazed and prostrated for returning consciousness to bring any immediate appreciation of her surroundings and what had befallen her.

Nolan did not speak, but waited patiently, knowing it then would be vain to question her.

The woman broke the silence. She seemed to be slowly grasping the situation, for she suddenly faltered vacantly, scarce above a whisper:

"Where am I?"

Nolan saw that she could not be moved immediately. He asked, a bit indifferently:

"Don't you know where you are?"

"No."

"Or how you came here?"

"No. I—"

"Wait a bit," Nolan interrupted. "Your head will clear in a few more minutes. Then you'll be able to tell me. What is your name? Can't you remember that?"

"Yes, of course," she replied, with more strength. "My name is Mary Waldmere."

"Ah!"

"I am Lady Waldmere, of—"

She broke off abruptly, starting up from the pillow, only to sink back again, too weak to rise. A frightened look in her eyes, however, told that she was beginning to remember.

"Where am I? Where is his lordship?" she cried, with lips quivering. "Why am I here? Who are you?"

"Hush!" Nolan cautioned. "Don't get excited, madam. It might not be good for you. Wait until you can recall all that happened to you. Then I'll see what can be done for—"

"Oh, oh, I remember—I remember it now!" cried Lady Waldmere, rising to her elbow. "I was seized and carried away by wicked men—and a woman! Tell me where I am. Tell me why I was brought here, and—"

"You calm yourself," Nolan interrupted, with some authority. "Keep cool and tell me the whole business. Do you know the men who brought you here?"

"No, no; I do not," moaned the woman.

"Or the woman who was with them?"

"No, nor the woman. She was veiled."

"How did they get away with you?"

"With the help of their chauffeur," Lady Waldmere brokenly explained. "He enticed me to the taxicab he was driving. I was told that a friend wished to see me. I did not know—did not suspect. I went with him to the taxicab door, leaving my husband waiting on the avenue."

"And then?" Nolan tersely questioned.

"There were two men and a woman in the taxicab," Lady Waldmere went on, quite hysterically. "The woman was veiled, as I told you. She held out her hand to me and I supposed that she knew me. I did not dream of anything wrong."

"Sure not," Nolan nodded.

"But when she grasped my hand, she seized it firmly and drew me into the taxicab. At the same time I felt the chauffeur push me from behind. I fell on the floor of the cab. One of the men seized me and held me, while the other covered my mouth with his hand."

"Brutes!"

"I nearly fainted," Lady Waldmere went on, moaning. "I knew, then, that I was being abducted. I tried to struggle and scream, when the taxicab sped away, but my efforts were futile. Then I felt a sharp pricking sensation in my shoulder—"

"The needle of a syringe," put in Nolan.

"I don't know—I don't know!" moaned the woman. "I know only that I fainted or lost consciousness. That is all I remember till now. I cannot tell who or why I—"

"One moment," said Nolan. "Were the men smooth shaved, or—"

"No, no! Both wore beards."

"They were in disguise."

"I cannot tell. I know only that I am in despair. I know—"

"Try to be calm," Nolan again interrupted. "Wait till you regain your strength. You then will be able to leave here, and—"

"Leave here?"

Lady Waldmere looked at him with a sudden wild hope leaping up in her tear-filled eyes.

"That's what I said," Nolan nodded.

"Do you mean—do you mean that you are not in the employ of my abductors?" Lady Waldmere asked, in faltering, frantic whispers. "Do you mean—"

"Oh, I'm in their employ, all right," Nolan dryly put in.

"Alas, then—"

"But not as you infer," Nolan added.

"Tell me what you do mean, then," entreated the woman, white and trembling. "Don't keep me in suspense. Am I to remain here and—"

"Not by a long chalk!"

"You will take me away? You will restore me to my husband?" Lady Waldmere's voice took on a hopeful ring. "Oh, I will pay you any sum if you will do so. Tell me—"

"Do you feel able to leave here?"

"Able—yes!"

"At once?"

"Heavens, man, yes!" Lady Waldmere started up from the bed. "But don't deceive me! I beg that you'll not deceive me. Will you take me away from here? Will you restore me to my husband? Will you—"

"You bet I will, madam!" cried Nolan. "That's what I'm here for."

"But if in the employ of those men—"

"Oh, that's another story," Nolan again interrupted, assisting the woman to rise. "I am also in the employ of your husband."

"My husband!"

"I am a detective. My name is Chick Carter."

The last was instantly taken up by a fierce, threatening voice in the adjoining hall.

"Throw up your hands, then, and keep them up! Let the woman alone—or you'll be a dead one!"

Chick swung round like a flash.

In the open doorway stood Morris Garland, with face as black as midnight and as threatening as his leveled weapon.

Behind him loomed the burly figure of a red-featured cabman, with blood in his eye and a blackjack in his hand.

Two other figures, those of women, were crouching against the wall farther down the hall—out of view of the startled detective.

# CHAPTER 7

## NICK CARTER'S DOINGS

It now is obvious, of course, that Chick Carter lied to Mr. Morris Garland—which was entirely warranted by the circumstances, since knavery can be successfully met only with its own weapons.

Nick Carter had turned only the nearest corner after leaving the quarters of the loan company, when he was overtaken by Chick, who, in reality, had been there only to note what followed Nick's visit with Waldmere, and to watch any move that either Garland or Hart might afterward make.

It so happened, however, owing to an unexpected opportunity afforded Chick, that their own respective designs were reversed.

"Well, what was doing?" Nick immediately questioned, when Chick hastened across the street and joined him. "I saw Hart talking to you through the window.

Chick hastily informed him, and Nick's face underwent a decided change.

"That does settle it," said he. "We have given them a fright, and now have them on the run. It's dollars to fried rings, now, that my suspicions are correct. It is necessary only to clinch them and nail all of the culprits involved in the game."

"What game?" asked Lord Waldmere curiously. "I'm jolly well mystified by this. Why—"

"Don't question," Nick interrupted. "Be patient, Waldmere, until I have got in my work. I then will answer all the questions you care to ask."

"But, hang it, old top, I—"

"You must do what I say," Nick cut in. "Time never was more valuable. One minute's delay may queer all of my work."

"What next?" Chick tersely asked, when Waldmere subsided.

"We'll change mounts," Nick replied pointedly. "Go ahead and keep the appointment with Garland. Meet him, as directed, though he'll not be likely to show up there for some little time, providing I rightly anticipate what's coming."

"What shall I tell him?"

"Tell him who I am," Nick directed. "Give it to him straight, in your own way, but only what will be consistent with your assumed character. Got me?"

"Dead to rights," Chick nodded.

"Be off, then, and I'll do the rest," said Nick. "I have left Patsy in the office, in case of sudden need. Call him up yourself, if occasion requires it."

Chick responded with another nod and hurried away.

"Now, Waldmere, you return to your lodgings," said Nick. "You will only be in my way, if you remain. Wait right there until I come."

"But—"

"Don't stop to question, dear fellow," Nick interrupted. "Every minute is of value."

"By Jove, I'm all at sea, don't you know, but here goes!" exclaimed his lordship, seeming suddenly to realize that he was indeed in the way.

He smiled with the last, nevertheless, and hurried across the street, presently vanishing around the nearest corner.

Nick Carter stepped into the corridor of a near building. The janitor, with a broom and a pail of rubbish, the result of his morning's cleaning, was just approaching a small store-room under the rise of stairs.

Nick overtook him at the open door.

"One moment, janitor," said he, stepping into the narrow room. "I am Nick Carter, the detective, and I'm on a rush case. Hang onto this cane and disguise until I call for them, will you? I then will make it worth your while."

"Sure, sor, I'm glad to do it," cried the janitor, eyes lighting. "Who don't know Nick Carter?"

"Good on your head," Nick nodded. "I want to reverse my trousers and coat, also, which will take but half a minute."

"Go ahead, sor. The room is yours for the asking."

Nick emerged from it in precisely thirty seconds, so changed in looks and attire, the latter expressly made to be quickly reversed, that he bore not even a remote resemblance to the man who had entered it. Then wearing no facial disguise, he again thanked the janitor and hurried away from the building, retracing his steps to Fifth Avenue.

Not more than five minutes had passed since he departed from the loan company office, when, from a doorway on the opposite side of the avenue, he was in a position to cautiously watch the place.

He had returned none too soon. He scarce had turned his gaze in that direction, when Garland came from the loan office in company with a handsome, flashily dressed woman of twenty-five, whom Nick had seen at a typewriter through the partly open door of Garland's private office.

"Garland's stenographer," he muttered. "I thought I recognized her, though she sat with her face averted. Vera Vantoon, eh? I have seen her with Stuart Floyd, of whom Chick was speaking last evening. She may be a connecting link in this chain. By Jove, they are off at a canter, for fair. On the run is right."

Garland and Vera Vantoon, a pronounced brunette with a striking face and figure, were hurrying up Fifth Avenue, evidently on as important a mission as the detective had been led to suspect.

Nick immediately followed them, though on the opposite side of the avenue.

They had covered less than two blocks, however, when an approaching taxicab swerved to the curbing and a man sprang out, who evidently had seen them from within the conveyance.

"By Jove, there's Stuart Floyd himself," thought Nick, stepping into a near doorway to watch them. "He was bound for Garland's office, as sure as I'm a foot high. I have forced the game, all right, plainly enough."

The last was occasioned by the earnest conference at once begun by the three, Garland doing most of the talking, and presently slipping a small cloth parcel into Floyd's coat pocket—a move undetected by Nick because of the intervening taxicab.

Floyd was an erect, splendidly built man with a smoothly shaved, clean-cut face, with regular features of an almost classic cast, an intellectual brow, and remarkably keen and expressive gray eyes. He was scrupulously well dressed and in strict accord with the dictates of fashion. He would readily have passed, as Chick had stated, for a millionaire or a prominent figure in the Gotham smart set. He was very well known, too, from Harlem to the Battery, though for more and varied reasons than any was yet led to suspect.

Nick saw plainly that he could not wisely undertake to overhear what the three were discussing so earnestly, nor did he attempt to do so. He knew very well, or thought he did, and was content to await what followed.

Nick had not long to wait. After an earnest conference lasting about five minutes, Garland and the woman entered the taxicab, which sped rapidly away, while Stuart Floyd walked briskly down the avenue.

"What's the meaning of that?" Nick asked himself. "They may have gone to make sure the abducted woman is still in safe keeping. Be that as it may, it's long odds that Floyd will rejoin them sooner or later. I have no course but to stick to him. I'll head him off, by Jove, and see what he will say for himself."

Nick did not immediately do so. He shadowed Floyd, instead, to one of the leading jewelry firms, who were large importers of diamonds and other gems, and through one of the broad plate windows he saw Floyd speak to the senior member of the firm and then retire with him to his private office.

Half an hour passed before Floyd emerged. He paused and shook hands with the merchant, bowing and smiling as if he had not a care on his mind, much less a burden, and he then left the store and walked briskly to a near hotel, entering the barroom and buying a drink.

Nick suspected what he was doing all the while, but he was not absolutely sure of it, and he continued the espionage. Passing through the hotel office to keep an eye on his quarry, he suddenly came face to face with Floyd in the adjoining corridor, the latter having just left the barroom.

It was an opportunity for which Nick had been waiting. He stepped directly in front of the man, saying familiarly:

"Hello! You're just the man I want to see, Mr. Floyd. Give me half a minute, will you?"

Floyd knew Nick Carter by sight. If he had seen a ghost, he would not have turned more pale for a moment. That he was a man of extraordinary nerve and self-possession, however, appeared in that, aside from his momentary paleness, not a feature of his clean-cut face evinced a sign of fear, or even secret perturbation.

"You are Mr. Carter, I believe," he replied, looking Nick straight in the eye.

"Yes."

"Why have you stopped me? What can I do for you?"

"Tell me what you know about the Imperial Loan Company," said Nick, straight from the shoulder.

Floyd heard him without a change of countenance.

"All that I know may be told with a single word—nothing," he replied.

"You know of the concern, don't you?"

"Yes."

"Are you acquainted with the managers?"

"Yes."

"Well acquainted?"

"So well acquainted, Mr. Carter, that I am not inclined to discuss them with any detective, not excluding yourself, before knowing the purpose of his inquiries," Floyd said coldly.

"If you know only good of them, Mr. Floyd, a detective is the very man with whom you should be most willing to discuss them," Nick retorted.

"I will not argue the point," Floyd said, flushing slightly.

"There is no occasion," said Nick. "Do you know anything about the inside workings of this loan company?"

"What do you mean, sir, by inside workings?"

"The methods they employ."

"I already have said, Carter, that I know nothing about them, aside from a personal acquaintance with the two managers," Floyd stiffly asserted. "Mr. Garland is a gentleman. Mr. Hart is another. That is all I can tell you."

"All that you will tell me, Mr. Floyd, is what you mean," Nick said pointedly. "You should have learned, nevertheless, that reticence is equivalent to—"

"Stop a moment," Floyd interrupted, with lips curling. "What's the big idea? What's it all about? Do you suspect the loan company of anything wrong?"

"Frankly, Mr. Floyd, I do," Nick nodded.

"Of what?"

"Of having abducted, or caused to be abducted, a woman known as Mrs. Archie Waldron. Did you ever hear of her?"

"Never! Permit me to add, Carter, that I never heard of anything more absurd."

"Than what?" questioned Nick, still sharply regarding him.

"Such a suspicion," snapped Floyd, his eyes dilating. "What earthly motive could they have for abducting a woman, or for any other breach of the law? Both are married and have families. Both are men of eminent respectability, of sterling integrity, and they manage a very profitable business. What earthly incentive could they have for committing crime? That's absurd, utterly improbable. You detectives go over the traces much too often, Carter, in your still-hunts after victims. You are worse in a way than the crooks, for you smirch the reputation of honorable men, while crooks get only their purses. Good morning, sir. That is all I have to say."

Floyd apparently had worked himself up to a state of righteous indignation, and none could better feign any sentiment he chose. He drew himself up and turned to go, but Nick detained him with a gesture.

"One moment," he replied. "You have said considerable, Floyd, for one who knew nothing about the Imperial Loan Company. I should be blind, indeed, if I did not see that. You extol them in order to divert my suspicions. But the fact that you think it is necessary to do so proves quite conclusively, not only that you know much more than you have stated, but also that my suspicions are correct. I could logically go even a step further, Floyd, and suspect you of being in their game."

Floyd's thin red lips parted scornfully, revealing a double row of sharp white teeth. It gave him for a moment the vicious expression of a dog about to bite. Instead, he vented a cold and mirthless laugh, as cold and mirthless as the ring from rapiers crossed in mortal combat.

"You go to thunder, Carter," said he, sneering contemptuously. "I would not lower myself by even denying your slanderous insinuations. In their game, or in any game—bah! You disgust me! Go to thunder!"

And Mr. Stuart Floyd, with the air and aspect of one who felt that he had squelched the famous detective, turned on his heel and entered the hotel office.

Nick Carter smiled and passed into the barroom.

"That will keep you going, all right," he said to himself. "That's all I want of you. I'll get you hands down at the finish."

# CHAPTER 8

## HOW NICK MADE GOOD

Nick Carter did not remain long in the barroom, only long enough to deftly put on a simple disguise, unobserved by any person in the room. He then passed out to the street and approached the hotel office—just as Stuart Floyd came out, departing quite hurriedly.

He walked by Nick, nearly touching him, but he did not recognize him. He glanced furtively into the barroom when passing it, nevertheless, which convinced Nick that he still was supposed to be there, and that his quarry was bent upon making a quick get-away.

Nick followed him cautiously, as before, noting that Floyd now appeared more hurried and apprehensive, but evidently not suspecting that he was being shadowed.

Floyd hastened over to Broadway, where he entered the quarters of the Crosstown Collateral Trust Company, one of the largest concerns of this kind in the country, if not in the world.

Nick watched him from outside.

Floyd appeared remarkably familiar with the place. He nodded to several of the clerks, waving his hand to the book-keeper, and at the same time he proceeded directly to the private office of the president of the company, which he entered without the formality of knocking.

Nick Carter's eyes took on a gleam of increasing satisfaction. He continued to wait and watch.

Presently a clerk hurried into the private office, evidently having been summoned. He emerged in a few moments and vanished into the business inclosure, where the doors of several huge vaults in the rear wall gave the place the appearance of a safety deposit, or a wealthy banking institution.

Five minutes later the same clerk again visited the private office, remaining only a moment, and half a minute later Floyd came out and started for the street.

Nick stole into a near doorway.

Floyd emerged in a moment and walked rapidly to a drug store on an opposite corner, proceeding directly to a telephone booth in the rear of the store, quickly entering and tightly closing the door.

Nick already was at the open door of the store. He saw that the booth stood in an angle formed by two of the counters. He saw, too, that there then were no customers and only one clerk in the store, just then engaged in wiping one of the show cases.

Nick stepped in and instantly caught the clerk's eye, though one of his own was constantly fixed upon the back of Floyd's head, visible through the window in the door of the booth. Floyd then was hurriedly looking up a number in the telephone-exchange book.

Nick cautioned the clerk with a significant glance and by holding up his forefinger. He then turned the lapel of his vest and displayed his detective's badge.

The clerk appeared to grasp the situation. He nodded and continued his work.

Nick stepped back of the opposite counter, quickly crouching out of sight behind it. He then crept to the rear of the store and within half a minute he was directly opposite one side of the telephone booth.

On hands and knees under the counter, he placed one ear against the side of the booth—and he then could faintly hear the voice of the man within.

The following broken remarks reached his ears, broken by the occasional responses from the person with whom Floyd was talking, whom the detective of course could not hear:

"There is no question about it," Floyd was forcibly saying. "I know positively that he is on the case…. Yes, yes, of course! But we can prevent that and bluff him to a standstill. He cannot prove that you know anything about her…. That's true, but I've got the goods and will show up shortly. The best way, then, will be to phone directly to his office and state where she can be found. That probably would end the matter, and there will be no way of telling from whom the information came. He could only guess at that…. The sooner the better, of course. I have hastened to notify you only to put you on your guard in case he shows up there again before I arrive. Stave him off in some way until I come. It then will be soft walking. I'll come at once. So long!"

Nick heard the sharp click of the hook when the receiver was replaced.

Floyd came from the booth almost immediately and left the store without so much as a glance at the clerk.

Nick crept from under the counter and entered the booth. He paused briefly to size up what he had heard. He felt sure Floyd had telephoned either to Hart, or Garland, at their place of business. He turned to the telephone and rang up his own business office.

"Line's busy!" called the exchange operator.

Nick waited.

"Who is on it?" he asked himself. "Patsy must be there. I directed him not to leave. Chick may have called him up, as I suggested, but for what reason? Hang this delay! It may prove expensive."

Nick tried again and succeeded. He heard the familiar voice of Patsy Garvan over the wire.

"This is the chief talking," said Nick.

"Oh, gee!" Patsy exclaimed. "I was just wondering how I could get next to you."

"What's up?" Nick questioned, deferring his own communication.

"Some one just phoned here that the woman we're seeking can be found at No. 1680B Amsterdam Avenue. The speaker evidently was a man, but I did not know his voice, nor could I get anything more from him."

"I can guess who," said Nick. "I was about to tell you that you would soon receive that information."

"What shall I do?"

"Take Danny and a couple of plain-clothes men to aid you," Nick quickly directed. "Raid the house quietly. I hardly think you will find any one else there. If you do, however, make sure that none escapes."

"Trust me for that."

"I'll nail the culprits elsewhere."

"Good enough! I've got you."

"That's all, then."

Nick came from the booth, said a few words of explanation to the astonished clerk, and he then hurriedly left the store and hailed a passing taxicab.

Ten minutes later, still in disguise, he entered the quarters of the Imperial Loan Company—not more than an hour after his visit with Lord Waldmere.

The first person he caught sight of was Moses Hart, and he saw at once that Stuart Floyd had not yet arrived.

The assistant manager, nevertheless, appeared much more at ease than an hour ago. He was engaged in the latticed inclosure. He was smiling and humming a popular air. He saw Nick approach one of the windows and he turned to meet him.

"Is Mr. Garland busy?" Nick blandly inquired, bowing and smiling.

"Mr. Garland is absent just now," Hart suavely rejoined.

"H'm, is that so?"

"I think he will return before noon," Hart added. "Is there anything I can do for you?"

"Are you the assistant manager?"

"I am."

"Perhaps, then, you will do as well, though Mr. Garland was mentioned to me," said Nick. "It's about a loan I wish to negotiate on some valuable jewelry. The amount is considerable, and—"

"Ah!"

Hart breathed an expressive sigh, one of avaricious anticipation, and he then hastened to open a door leading into the inclosure.

"Walk in, sir," he said cordially. "Step into our private office. We then can discuss the matter without interruptions."

Nick was waiting only for an interruption.

"Oh, I don't think that will be necessary," he demurred. "I can tell you briefly what I require."

"Very well."

Hart stepped out and joined him.

"My name is Peterson," Nick continued. "I have in my charge a quantity of valuable jewelry. It is part of the estate of a very wealthy widow. The estate has not been settled, owing to long litigation, and it has become necessary to raise quite a sum of cash with which to meet legal expenses."

"I follow you," Hart nodded, anticipating an unusually profitable deal.

"I may require ten thousand dollars, possibly more."

"What is the value of the jewelry?"

"Fifty thousand, at least."

"Ah! In that case, Mr. Peterson, we will be delighted to accommodate you," Hart warmly assured him. "No loan is too large for us to make on satisfactory collateral. Our capital is unlimited. We can refer you to—"

He broke off abruptly.

Stuart Floyd had entered and was hurriedly approaching.

"One moment, Hart!" he exclaimed, diving into his coat pocket and failing to recognize Nick. "Excuse yourself for one moment. Here is that package which—"

"Let me have it, instead," Nick interrupted, thrusting Hart aside.

Floyd recoiled as if struck on the head.

"You!" he gasped involuntarily.

Nick whipped off his disguise.

"Yes," he said sternly. "I may need it to prove my case—and your relations with the Imperial Loan Company. Let me have it."

Floyd staggered and then uttered a cry and pulled himself together.

"Not by a long shot!" he shouted. "Get rid of this, Hart, before he can learn what it—"

But he got no further, for Nick Carter did not stand on ceremony. He leaped at Floyd and wrenched the package from him, as the latter was about to toss it to Hart, and then he forced him fiercely against the wall.

Then came the jingle and snapping of steel—and Floyd was in handcuffs.

"Let those keep you quiet," said Nick sharply. "I think, now, we are in a fair way to settle this business—and settle it right!"

# CHAPTER 9

## THE LOOTING GAME

The situation in which Chick Carter suddenly found himself with Lady Waldmere was not an enviable one. Without knowing just how it had come about, Chick realized on the instant that he was caught like a rat in a corner, the interior room having no window, nor any way of egress save through the door, then barred by the tall figure and threatening weapon of Morris Garland, to say nothing of the burly cabman behind him.

Chick was not blind, however, to one offsetting advantage the room afforded, or might possibly be made to afford. If he could escape only through the door, he also could be attacked only from that direction.

Chick took that in on the instant, also, and he was in no mood to yield submissively to the two threatening miscreants in the hall.

He threw up his hands, nevertheless, while a shriek of terror came from Lady Waldmere—both sufficient to throw Garland off his guard for the fraction of a second.

Instantly Chick took advantage of it.

Without dropping his hands, lest the knave might shoot, Chick raised his right foot under one of the rounds of the chair on which he had been seated, then kicked it with all his strength straight at the open door.

It went direct and went like a flash.

It struck Garland squarely on the arm and breast, diverting his aim, and then fell to the floor.

Garland fired on the instant, nevertheless, and the bullet went into the ceiling.

Lady Waldmere uttered another shriek and fainted dead away on the bed.

The deafening report of the weapon was instantly followed by the bang of Chick's revolver, whipped like a flash from his hip pocket.

In his haste, however, he had fired almost at random. The bullet clipped a lock of hair from Garland's head, then passed within an inch of the cabman's ear.

Both uttered a yell. Both leaped instinctively, as it were, to one side of the open door, bringing the wall between them and the detective.

That was all that Chick wanted at that moment, and he had accomplished it by taking his life in his hand.

He now laughed aloud, however, and cried:

"Two can play at that game, you see. If either of you rats shows his head at the door, I'll not miss it with my next bullet."

This brought no response for a moment.

Chick heard the two men whispering in the hall, and also the rustle of skirts.

"By Jove, there may have been another woman in the house when I stole in," he said to himself, constantly alert. "She may have heard me, or saw me, and afterward sent word to Garland. That may be how they caught me in this fashion."

Chick's theory was quite nearly correct. As a matter of fact, a sister of Vera Vantoon, who had figured in the episode in the taxicab, had been left in the hurriedly rented furnished house, rented expressly after the abduction had been accomplished, in order that the identity of none of the culprits should afterward be discovered.

This sister, Leah Vantoon, had seen Chick stealing into the house. She later had stolen out and got word to Garland, happening to meet Vera and the chauffeur, then on their way to the house. All of them had stolen in and up the stairs, unheard by the detective, while Chick was talking with Lady Waldmere.

Morris Garland had, of course, then realized how craftily he had been duped by Nick Carter himself.

He did not realize it all, however, for Stuart Floyd and Moses Hart were at that moment under arrest by the famous detective.

Chick's taunting remark was answered in a few seconds by Garland.

At the same moment, too, Chick saw that Lady Waldmere had revived and was sitting on the edge of the bed. He held up his finger, warning her to be silent, then signed for her to seek a remote corner of the room, where a bullet from the hall could not possibly hit her.

He, in the meantime, remained crouching some six feet from the open door, revolver in hand.

"I say!" called Garland, from the hall.

"Say ahead," called Chick coolly. "Come on with it."

"You'd better quit and throw up your hands again," Garland advised.

"May they wither, Garland, if I do," replied Chick. "If you cannot think of anything better to say, you'd better keep quiet."

"Oh, we'll get you finally."

"Is that so?"

"You bet it's so. There is no way for you to get out."

"Nor for you to get in," Chick retorted.

"We can starve you out."

"Not much."

"Think not, eh?"

"I know it," Chick declared confidently. "Before you could do that, Garland, the entire police force will be in search of me. They'll find me, too."

"Why do you think so?"

"Because your running mate in the game you have been playing will throw up his hands and squeal," Chick asserted. "He probably is under arrest by this time."

"By whom?" Garland demanded incredulously.

"By Nick Carter."

"I guess not. What do you mean by the game we've been playing?"

"Nick knows. He suspected it from the first."

"Knows what?"

Chick laughed and clicked the revolver suggestively.

"Don't come any nearer that door, Garland, or there'll be something doing," he advised. "I wouldn't shrink an instant from sending a bullet into your block of solid ivory. We've got your game down pat, now, and we're going to get you."

"What game?" Garland again demanded. "What do you mean?"

"Your looting game," said Chick. "That's a good name for it, too. You two rascals, evidently with others to help you, have taken advantage of the fact that the head of the business you only manage, Mr. Isaac Meyer, is a helpless paralytic and confined to his home."

"How taken advantage?"

"You have been looting his business of all that it would stand without immediate detection," said Chick. "You have been loaning small amounts on gems and jewels and the like, and then pawning the collateral elsewhere for a much larger sum, and whacking up the difference. When a customer shows up to redeem a pledge, if it happens to be one that you have put elsewhere, you stave him off until you can raise the dust to redeem it yourselves, in case you don't have it on hand, that you may turn it over to the proper owner and thus avert exposure. But it's bound to come, Garland; it's bound to come. In fact, it already is here."

"That's what Nick Carter suspects, is it?"

Garland spoke with a sneer, but his voice had a quaking uncertainty that told of utter dismay, of a realization that he had played a losing game and must pay the price.

"Sure that's what he suspects," Chick replied complacently. "You're a bunch of star looters, that's what you are. When the books and vaults of the Imperial Loan Company are examined, you'll be found to be a hundred thousand short, at least."

"Confound you Carters, anyway!" Garland cried, with a snarl. "You know too much."

"Too much for most crooks whom we get after," Chick dryly admitted.

"It may cost you something one of these days."

"It already has cost you something," Chick retorted. "Nick tumbled to it almost off the reel. You were in pressing peril when the woman unexpectedly showed up to redeem her ten-thousand-dollar pledge. You have shoved up the jewels somewhere else, and probably for fifteen or twenty thousand. You did not have the jewels when she called yesterday, nor the money with which to redeem them this morning. Nick suspected it, Garland, and we got right at you to drive you to the wall. We have done it, all right."

Chick heard a growl from the cabman, one Buck Morgan, who had driven the taxicab the previous afternoon, and Chick also heard the remark that followed it.

"The cursed dick is right, Morris. We'd better make a quick get-away."

"Not on your life," snarled Garland. "I'll get him first, or—hark! What was that?"

There was little need to ask, nor had Morgan any time in which to answer the question.

The hurried tread of several men sounded in the lower hall and then on the near stairway. They came rushing up at top speed, Patsy Garvan in the lead.

"It's all off, Mr. Garland; all off!" he shouted, while he came, at the same time brandishing a ready revolver. "Don't attempt any funny business, or there'll be a dead pawnbroker here. Shut up, you two women, or we'll put you in irons with these two gazabos."

The raid, quietly made, indeed, as Nick had directed, was already a success. Both Garland and Morgan collapsed the moment they saw Patsy and the other detectives. They were capable of thieving and abduction, but not of murder and bloodshed.

Within five minutes Patsy had all four of the culprits in irons, and in five more they were on their way to the Tombs, to which Stuart Floyd and Hart already had preceded them.

Half an hour later Lady Waldmere was restored to the arms of her anxious husband, who, it seems needless to say, was jolly well pleased.

It later appeared that all of Nick Carter's suspicions, as set forth in brief by Chick, were entirely correct. Nick had felt reasonably sure of it from the first, but knew that he must secure absolute proof of it, which he set about doing in the manner described.

He knew that Garland and Hart would have to work lively to raise the money to recover the Waldmere jewels, that they might be turned over to her that morning, and that that was Garland's mission when he left his office with Vera Vantoon, afterward meeting Floyd.

That the latter then had undertaken the mission, and that he was in league with the others, became obvious to Nick when Floyd visited the jewelry firm. He rightly reasoned that Garland had provided him with a parcel of diamonds, or other costly gems, from those in pawn with the loan company, upon which Floyd could obtain a loan from the jeweler. It afterward was shown to be eighteen thousand dollars.

That Floyd then went and redeemed the jewels from the Crosstown Collateral Trust Company. Nick had not had a doubt, and he shaped his course accordingly, meeting with complete success and later showing that Mr. Isaac Meyer had, indeed, been almost utterly ruined by his treacherous managers.

"They now will get theirs," Nick observed, speaking of the case that evening. "I have no doubt that Floyd was the genius back of the whole job, but we may not be able to prove even that. However, be that as it may, it was very quick work, cleaned up within twenty-four hours."

"Yes, chief," supplemented Patsy. "And as his blooming English nobs would say, and has said—deucedly keen and clevah work, bah Jove, deucedly keen and clevah!"

www.ingramcontent.com/pod-product-compliance
Lightning Source LLC
Chambersburg PA
CBHW020642130626
46552CB00003B/1352